寬背馬阿肥的馬術輔助治療記

文/孟瑛如
圖/閻寧
英文翻譯/吳侑達

我生長在純種馬的家族，卻有著寬背。

我們家是有名的賽馬家族，我的兄弟姊妹跟親戚得過無數賽馬獎盃。賽馬的體型要纖細精實，加速能力要好，但我跑步時不愛隨意加速，更不喜歡前面有一堆障礙物等著我跨越！

我喜歡沉思，喜歡慢慢散步，喜歡有人輕輕撫摸我，而不是拿鞭子抽打我！

我喜歡安靜的場合，不想要有很多人在旁邊喧囂叫鬧，揮舞一堆彩票，像發瘋似的叫著我的名字！

　　我長大到接近兩歲時，被移到了另一間馬房。在這裡，馬房管理員達達每天都應接不暇的接待來自各方的練馬師到馬廄選馬。

　　我看著他們來來去去，極少有練馬師會在我的馬廄前停留。練馬師常常因為我不夠纖細精實、因為我的寬背及溫和的個性而一眼就斷定我不會是匹好賽馬。

一天，有個練馬師開玩笑的跟另一位練馬師說：「千萬別選那匹馬，他看起來就是一副阿肥樣！」「寬背？但為什麼不是長得像吉普賽馬那般夢幻飄逸？不然還可以去馬展供人觀賞或是讓新人騎著拍婚紗照。」這也是我很想知道的答案啊！

　　沒想到在你一言我一語的傳播下，「阿肥」就成了我的名字。每天的選馬活動，我既無處可去，又不會被練馬師選上，這些都讓我覺得自己像在船上跑馬般，只有「走投無路」四個字可以形容。

　　馬房管理員達達是我最好的人類朋友。每到黃昏時分，當我又經歷了一天的失望，他總會溫和的拍拍我，告訴我說：「不急，欣賞我們的人只是還沒出現！」「我們有權利做最好的自己！」

　　「每一件事，可能都需要不只一次的勇氣。我們可以鼓勵自己有第一次的勇氣，也可以鼓勵自己有第二次、第三次的勇氣去等待欣賞我們的伯樂！」達達對我說。

　　我覺得達達很像哲學家，總是能針對事情說出一番道理，又很能安撫我。連我僅是露出疑惑的表情，猜想達達為何只要當一名馬房管理員，他都彷彿可以讀我的心般，立刻笑著說：「為什麼不呢？我從小就很喜歡馬，現在可以每天跟你們在一起，還有人付我薪水呢！興趣能和工作結合，這是老天爺厚待我啊！」

　　希望有一天我也能像達達一樣，活得如此達觀又自在。

日子一天天過去，我的兄弟姊妹都有了自己專屬的練馬師及騎馬師，有的兩歲就去比賽，最遲在三或四歲也都出去比賽了。他們都有一個很酷的名字，像「賽神」、「得勝」、「先鋒」、「幸運」等。他們每天的對話都是：「只要有我在，一定會馬到成功，哈哈哈！」「我總是一馬當先！」「我已經贏比賽贏到想要改名叫『獨孤求敗』了！」「我幫主人不知賺了多少錢呢！」

當他們一個個踏上成功之路，只有我還叫做阿肥，什麼都不是，只能默默的在馬廄裡獨自沉思。

　　有一天，達達帶來一位和藹的中年男子，直接站在我的馬廄前，這是前所未有的情況，我的心臟興奮得怦怦跳，直覺到有什麼美好的事即將發生在自己身上！中年男子說：「我要的馬是要做馬術輔助治療的，所以頸部到背部的曲線要平順，背肌要厚實，動作協調性要佳。」背肌要厚實！那不就是我嗎？選我！選我！我的眼睛熱切的直視著他，希望他能看見我的渴望！

中年男子繼續說：「馬術輔助治療並不會要求騎馬者駕馭馬匹，而是要讓騎馬者跟隨馬的步伐律動，做身體重心位置移動及姿勢控制反應。」他講得有點難懂，但我知道意思是不會用馬鞭催促我快跑，只要我好好的走。這真是太棒了！

「我們服務的對象通常是需要長期復健的身心障礙人士以及小朋友，尤其是小朋友若可以接觸到動物，就會對治療特別有興趣。他們常常覺得馬術輔助治療的馬就像是電影《阿凡達》裡的恐龍坐騎呢！」「所以我要的馬要寬背，喜歡跟人親近，要有耐心、可靠而且溫和的！」

　　聽到他們說的話，我真的太開心了，原來我這麼有特色，不再是別人眼中不夠纖細精實，加速不夠快的阿肥，我就是我！

　　達達在我的耳朵旁輕輕對我說：「你的伯樂出現了，去做你該做的事吧！散步就是你的興趣，再沒有比這更適合你的工作了！」我所堅持的第 N 次勇氣，終於有了好回饋！

　　一進到馬術輔助治療場，我都還分不清誰是馬術教練、誰是物理治療師、領馬員等，就聽到一堆人大叫：「天啊！你去哪裡找來這麼棒的馬！背好平滑結實，看起來還有張笑臉呢！」「他自己靠過來讓我摸呢！個性一定不錯！」「阿肥？這麼可愛的名字，小朋友一定會喜歡！他天生就是吃這行飯的！」聽得我飄飄然，原來放對位置就是「馬」才，放錯了位置，什麼「才」都不是！

　　俗話說：「人靠衣裳馬靠鞍。」但我不用像其他兄弟姊妹背著厚重的鞍，只要寬背上鋪張毯子就可以騎，因為這樣才能讓騎馬者真正與我的律動一致。人類成年人的走路步伐頻率大約是一分鐘110到120步，我在慢走時也差不多是這樣的頻率呢！

聽說我的骨盆律動與人類走路時的骨盆運動是很相似的,所以我每天只要慢慢走路就好了,而且額頭前面還會掛著一根我最愛吃的胡蘿蔔!

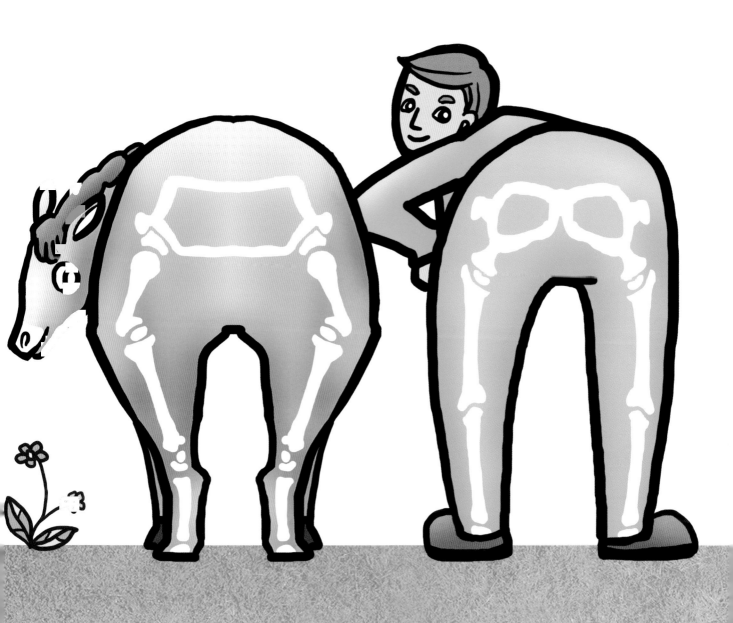

　　我每次只要走個30分鐘就會超過3000步，騎在我背上的人就會有上千次的機會練習身體重心位置移動及姿勢控制反應，這樣可以改善他們的平衡感及協調性，也可以增加關節活動度和肌肉的力量。

　　我現在覺得散步散得好可以幫助人類是件很有意義的工作，而且每次散步結束，眼前那根甜美的胡蘿蔔就會滑進我嘴裡當作獎勵！

　　馬術教練對我很好，他總是輕輕摸摸我，對我說：「你的寬背及好性情真是上天給你的最好禮物！」「因為你有點壯，我起先還擔心你會讓腦性麻痺的小朋友像是矮子騎大馬，上下為難呢！沒想到你這麼棒！」

我現在是馬術輔助治療中心裡的閃亮明星了，馬術教練要我走的長短交替步伐，或是走圓形、∞字型等全都難不倒我！

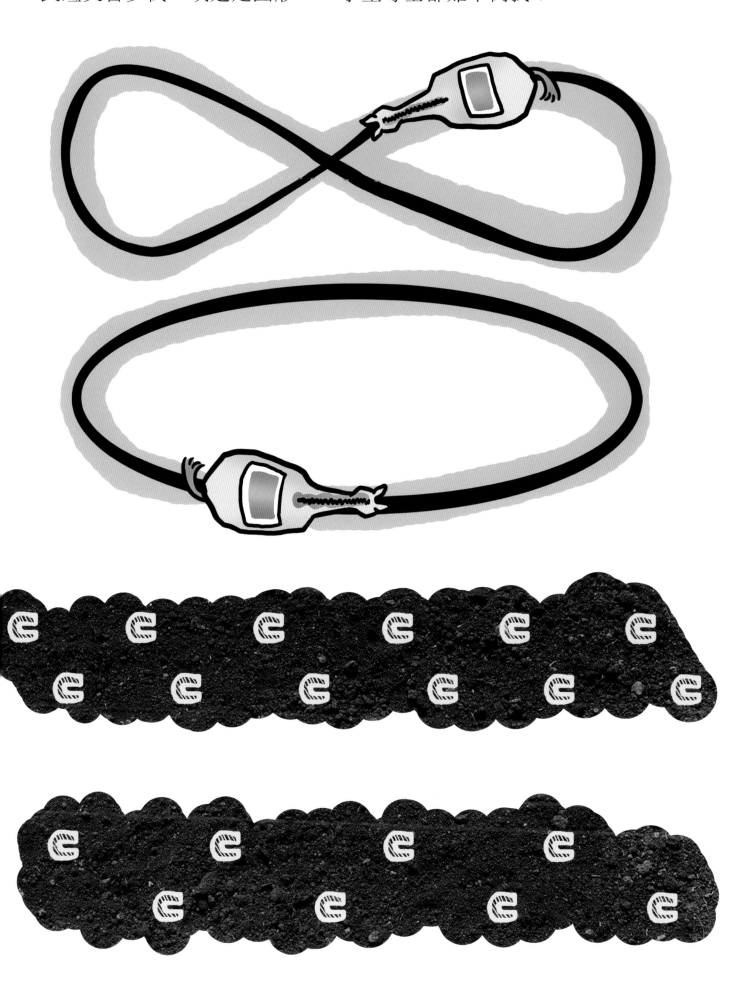

我有一大群來做治療的腦性麻痺小朋友粉絲，我只要轉動我靈活的耳朵，遠遠就可以聽到他們努力想叫出我名字的聲音！我現在覺得「阿肥」這個名字好可愛！

許多腦麻小朋友們的四肢僵直或捲曲到無法好好伸展，但他們在做完治療後，仍努力的想摸摸我表達謝意，而我總是把毛茸茸的頭盡量放低，這是我能享受到最真誠的溫柔與關懷！

謝謝你們，讓我感覺到自己的存在，讓我懂得真正的愛。這份特別的愛要給特別的你們！

希望你們也和我一樣，總是擁有第二次、第三次、……第 N 次的勇氣，找到屬於自己尊嚴自主的人生！

• 給教師及家長的話 •

　　筆者會寫這本《寬背馬阿肥的馬術輔助治療記》，首先要感謝財團法人腦性麻痺基金會何麗梅理事長及台北市學習障礙者家長協會劉永寧理事長，是他們兩人邀我去中壢的台灣馬術治療中心，讓我接觸了這一群安靜自得、溫和堅持服務我們身心障礙孩子的馬天使。更要感謝台灣馬術治療中心張兆遠教練提供馬天使的照片，這讓我決定要將照片附在繪本內，希望能讓讀者看看這些馬天使的真正面容與姿態──牠們有的慧黠、有的敦厚，更多的是寬容與愛！同時要感謝台灣馬術治療中心裡的工作人員，在台灣馬術輔助治療的道路上他們是先驅，而這也是一條寂寞的路，謝謝他們一路走來，始終堅持不懈！

　　許多身障孩子要適應社會都需要第二次、第三次，甚或是第 N 次的勇氣去嘗試，但是真實世界裡其實不會有人在乎你跌倒多少次，只要你站起來的次數再多一次就可以了。在這本繪本裡，我嘗試結合主角寬背馬阿肥被選擇到馬場做馬術輔助治療前的挫折經驗，與後來充滿成就感的快樂做對照，希望能介紹給大家有關馬術輔助治療在特殊教育界的應用，並且藉由寬背馬阿肥的永遠樂觀等待與堅持嘗試的生活態度，鼓勵身障孩子永遠要有再一次的勇氣。或許我們離成功只有一步之遙而不自知，也或許我們生命中的貴人近在咫尺，而我們未曾珍惜，生活中有無限的可能，只要我們能堅持跌倒後一定要想辦法站起來，總有一天，我們會遇見屬於自己的幸福！

寬背馬的英姿

感謝 ❤ 台灣馬術治療中心張兆遠教練及財團法人腦性麻痺基金會提供馬匹照片

The Story of Fatty:
A Horse with an Unusually Long, Wide Back

Written by Ying-Ru Meng
Illustrated by Ning Yan
Translated by Arik Wu

Though I am a member of a Thoroughbred family, I look nothing like average thoroughbred horses. They have short backs. I, however, have a long, wide back.

My siblings and relatives are all famous race-horses, as they have won numerous medals in different races. They are lean, agile, and good at accelerating.

I am different. When I canter, I do not like to accelerate every once in a while, nor do I like the feeling of seeing many obstacles waiting ahead of me.

I like musing over philosophical questions. I like strolling. I like people touching me gently, instead of whipping me fiercely. I like places that are quiet, not where crowds of people put their lotteries in the air, waving, yelling, and chanting my name as if crazy.

I am sent to another stable when I am about to turn two. There, Da Da, the stable keeper, receives horse trainers from around the world who wish to find horses suitable for further training every day.

I watch as they come and go, never stopping by my stall to give me a closer look. They do not see me as a good racehorse, I think, because I am neither lean nor aggressive enough. What is worse, I have a back that is unusually long and wide.

One day, two trainers come to visit our stable. One of them says to the other, "Do you see that horse out there? Looks just like a fatty! Look, he has a wide back, but why isn't he as divinely beautiful as the Gypsy Vanner horses? If he is, he can at least be of some use in horse shows or wedding photo shoots." Well, why am I not as beautiful as other horses? I want an answer as well!

The news that there is a weirdly looking horse in the stable spreads pretty fast. "Fatty" soon becomes my nickname. At this point, I feel like my life has reached a dead end. I have literally nowhere to go because it is obvious that not a single trainer wants me.

So far, Da Da has been my best human friend. Every day when the sun sets, I always feel extremely disappointed because I am once again left unselected. He always pats me on the back, and says, "It's okay. The one who truly appreciates us hasn't shown up yet, but don't lose faith just because of that. We have the right to be the best of ourselves!"

"Even if we fail once, twice, or thrice, that's alright, we can always give it another try. We should always be positive that the one who truly understands our true worth will find us one day," Da Da says.

Da Da sounds very much like a philosopher, I think. He can always make sense out of everything, and soothe and tranquilize my mind effortlessly. I once looked at Da Da curiously, wondering why he always seems satisfied with only being a stable keeper. Surprisingly, he seemed to understand what I wanted to ask. "Why not? Horses always fascinate me, and I love to be with you. You know what? I think I'm very lucky to have people pay me to do what I love," he said a smile on his face.

How I wish I could be as optimistic and positive!

Up until now, my siblings have all got their personal trainers and jockeys. For them, entering horse racing at the age of two, or even three or four, is pretty normal. Also, they all have names that sound really cool, such as "Unbeatable," "Victorious," "Vanguard" and "Luckiest."

"Ha! I'm just unbeatable!" "I always outrun other horses!" "I'm killing it in those races! When will I ever get a loss?" "I've won millions of dollars for my master!" They are always in a heated discussion.

Alas! While they are on their way to success, I, Fatty, am still a nobody that has nothing better to do. All I can do is musing over things in the stable. Alone, of course.

One day, Da Da, along with a kind-looking, middle-aged man, come to the front of my stall. This never happened before, so I can totally feel my heart pounding within my chest. I am sure something wonderful is about to happen!

"I'm looking for a horse to help me conduct hippotherapy. This horse has to be physically coordinated and have a back that is both strong and easy to ride on," the man says.

A back that is strong and wide? Is he talking about me? Me! Choose me! Choose me! I look right at him without looking away, hoping that he will see how badly I want to be chosen!

"So, when we do the therapy, we don't ask riders to direct horses. Instead, riders need to adjust their posture and balance according to different movements of their horses," the middle-aged man explains.

What he just said is a bit hard to grasp, but I am positive that no whip will be used during the therapy. I can stroll as much as I like. Wonderful!

"We usually serve children and disabled individuals to relax and rehabilitate. Children in general are excited about receiving the therapy because they get to interact with horses. They often feel that the horses used in the therapy are just like the Ikrans in the movie *Avatar*. So I'm looking for a horse that not only has a wide back, but also gets along with people well. Also, this horse needs to be patient, reliable, and even-tempered," he says.

It is truly delightful to know that my traits are actually appreciated! So, it turns out that I am, in fact, very unique! I am no longer the "less lean, agile, and slower one in the herd"! I am who I am!

Da Da leans over to speak softly into my ear, "Now, that's the person who truly understands your true worth! Do what you should do. Isn't strolling your habit? I think this is the best job for you!"

My perseverance has finally paid off!

The middle-aged man then takes me to the therapeutic riding center he works at. There are already a number of people there. I do not know which ones of them are trainers, physical therapists, or riding instructors, but I can hear they shout in amazement. "My goodness! Where did you find such a fine horse? He has a back that is so strong and easy to ride on! See! He's even smiling!"

"Hey, you see, he approaches me himself to let me pat on his back. He must be a very friendly horse," one of them says. "Is his name 'Fatty'? What a lovely name! I bet kids will love him very much. He is born to be doing this, I am sure," another one of them says.

I am so flattered and feel like I am on cloud nine! Now, I see that a horse being put in a wrong position is simply nothing, but if this horse gets to play to his strengths, he or she can be very, very successful.

People often say that clothing defines a person, and saddles define a horse. However, as a therapeutic horse, I do not need to burden myself with heavy saddles like my siblings do. I only need to put a blanket on my back, so as to allow riders to really respond to the rhythm of my movements. A human adult takes around 110 to 120 steps in a minute. When strolling, I take roughly the same number of steps per minute as well!

Also, based on what I heard from other people before, the pelvic movement of a horse when walking is similar to that of a human. So, all I need to do every day is simply strolling around. What is even better, there is always a carrot dangling in front of me. I love it!

I can take more than 3,000 steps every 30 minutes, which means a rider will have over a thousand opportunities to practice controlling his or her posture and shifting weight during a therapeutic session, and further improve his or her physical coordination and balance.

I now see that just strolling around can actually help many people! This job is really, really meaningful! Better yet, every time I finish a session, I will get that carrot dangling in front of me slide down my throat as a reward. Yummy!

My trainer treats me very well. He always pats me softly on the back and says, "Your long, wide back and friendliness are truly the grace of God. At first, I thought a horse of your size would give those children with cerebral palsy a hard time, but it seems that you're the perfect fit!"

Now, I am the star of the therapeutic riding center. It does not matter if it is walking in circle, doing the infinity walks, or switching between big and small steps, I can handle them all!

A lot of children love me very much. Every time when I shake my ears back and forth nimbly, they, though with cerebral palsy, will try their best to pronounce my name. Oh, "Fatty"! I now think this is a lovely, lovely name!

When each therapeutic session draws to an end, those children always come up to me, trying their best to pat me with their physically challenged hands, as a sign of gratitude. I, in response, always try to lower my fluffy head to make it easier for them to touch me. This has truly been the most heartfelt love I have ever felt!

Thank you all for making me feel alive and loved. Now, I know what love really is, and I especially want to share it with every one of you.

I hope you understand that it is OK to fail a couple of times, because we can always give it another try after each failure. Just keep on trying. Eventually, you will lead a life of dignity and independence!